5-MINUTE STAR WARS VILLAIN STORIES

Disney

LUCASFILM

PRESS

LOS ANGELES • NEW YORK

Collection © & TM 2017 Lucasfilm Ltd.

"Yoda and the Count" written by Rebecca L. Schmidt

"Escape from Darth Vader" written by Brooke Dworkin and illustrated by Stephane Roux

"The Battle of Hoth" written by Calliope Glass

"Rescue from Jabba's Palace" written by Brooke Dworkin

"Chaos at the Castle" written by S. T. Bende

Unless otherwise noted, all illustrations by Pilot Studio

This special edition was printed for Kohl's Department Stores, Inc. (for distribution on behalf of Kohl's Cares, LLC, its wholly owned subsidiary), by Disney • Lucasfilm Press, an imprint of Disney Book Group, Los Angeles/New York.

Kohls
Style Number 9781368022880
Factory Number 131635
07/17–09/17

Printed in the United States of America

First Hardcover Edition, September 2017

10 9 8 7 6 5 4 3 2 1

FAC-038091-17268

ISBN 978-1-368-02288-0

Visit the official *Star Wars* website at: www.starwars.com.

CONTENTS

A long time ago in a galaxy far, far away. . . .

YODA AND THE COUNT

Jedi Master Yoda was one of the leaders of the Jedi Order. He was wise and knew many things. Above all, Yoda believed in the Force. But now Yoda sensed a great disturbance in the Force. Count Dooku, Yoda's old apprentice, was trying to raise an army against Yoda and the other Jedi Knights!

The Jedi's search for Dooku led them to the planet Geonosis. A great battle broke out, and Dooku tried to escape. But Yoda's companions, Obi-Wan Kenobi and Anakin Skywalker, raced after him. Yoda sensed the presence of his powerful old apprentice and followed the two young Jedi to a small hangar bay far away from the battle.

When Yoda entered the hangar, he saw Obi-Wan and Anakin hurt and on the ground. Standing over them was the evil Count Dooku!

Count Dooku glared at the Jedi. "Master Yoda," he said.

"Count Dooku," Yoda said. He knew that he had to stop Dooku to protect his two friends. He also knew that there was still a chance to stop the battle on Geonosis before it became a war.

"You have interfered with our affairs for the last time!" Dooku said as he used the Force to rip objects off the walls, then throw them straight at Yoda.

But Yoda knew Dooku's tricks and was prepared. He used the Force to swat Dooku's missiles aside. Frustrated, Dooku tried to bring the ceiling down on the small Jedi Master, but Yoda was too strong for him. He pushed the rocks away.

"Powerful you have become, Dooku," Master Yoda told the Count.

"I have become more powerful than any Jedi. Even you," Dooku replied. With that, the Count raised his hand and shot Force lightning at his old Jedi Master!

But Yoda refused to be afraid. He used the Force to bend the lightning up and away from him. Count Dooku could only watch in astonishment! He tried again, but this time Yoda closed his fist around the lightning until it disappeared!

"Much to learn you still have," Yoda told Count Dooku.

"It is obvious that this contest cannot be decided by our knowledge of the Force but by our skills with a lightsaber," the Count said as he raised his red lightsaber. Yoda called his own to his hand. Its green blade glowed as he lifted it to fight Count Dooku.

Yoda and Count Dooku leapt
across the room at each other. Their
lightsabers cut through the air. Yoda
circled around the Count, his blade
flying—always one step ahead
of Dooku. The two blades
crackled against each other,
and Yoda forced Count
Dooku back.

The Count was amazed as Yoda jumped high across the hangar to land smoothly back down in front of him. Dooku realized he wasn't powerful enough to beat Yoda.

"Fought well, you have, my old Padawan," Yoda told the Count.

"This is just the beginning," Dooku said. And then he smiled, because he had discovered a way to win the fight.

Count Dooku raised his hand, and a huge tower began to crash down toward the defenseless Obi-Wan and Anakin! Count Dooku gave Yoda the choice between capturing him and saving the lives of his fellow Jedi. For Yoda there was no choice. He dropped his lightsaber and raised both hands to stop the column from falling on his friends. He could sense Count Dooku escaping to his ship.

There was now no chance for peace, but Yoda trusted in the Force. Count Dooku thought that the dark side was a shortcut to victory, but Yoda knew that the Count's victory would not last long. The Force was more powerful than Dooku could even imagine, and with it Yoda and his friends would one day defeat the dark side.

STAR WARS

ESCAPE FROM DARTH VADER

It was a time of war. Rebel spies fought the sinister Empire for control of the galaxy.

One of the rebels was named Princess Leia. She had been given plans for the Empire's newest weapon—the Death Star. Now Leia was on her starship, heading home to Alderaan. But she was not alone. An Imperial ship was chasing her!

On board Leia's ship were two droids: R2-D2 and C-3PO.

C-3PO was worried. He did not like being attacked!

"We're doomed," he said as the starship shook. "There'll be no escape for the princess this time!"

Suddenly, a loud blast rocked the ship. It had been captured!

As the droids watched, the starship's main door blasted open. Stormtroopers rushed through, swarming the ship.

The stormtroopers fired their blasters at the rebels, and the rebels fired back. One by one the rebels fell. Soon the stormtroopers were in full control of the ship.

As the battle wound down, a mysterious figure emerged from the smoke. It was Darth Vader.

In the commotion, R2-D2 slipped away. Noticing that R2-D2 was missing, C-3PO set out to find his friend. "Artoo-Detoo, where are you?" he called.

Elsewhere on the ship, Princess Leia looked at the plans for the Death Star. She knew she had to keep them safe. If the Empire got the plans back, the rebels wouldn't stand a chance!

Just then, R2-D2 appeared. That gave Princess Leia an idea.

Princess Leia leaned over and began speaking to the droid. She was recording a message for someone who she hoped could help her and the Rebel Alliance.

"I have placed information vital to the survival of the Rebellion into the memory systems of this Artoo unit," she explained.

When Princess Leia was done with her message, she inserted the plans for the Death Star into R2-D2. Then she told him where to go.

Princess Leia was just finishing her instructions when C-3PO found R2-D2.

"At last," he said. "Where have you been?" C-3PO pointed back at the stormtroopers. "They're heading in this direction. What are we going to do?"

But R2-D2 wasn't listening. He turned around and zipped off toward the escape pods.

Princess Leia watched until she was sure R2-D2 was safe. Then, lifting her hood over her head, she crept into the shadows. There was still a chance she could get away, too!

Meanwhile, Darth Vader was speaking to one of his commanders.

"The Death Star plans are not in the main computer," the commander reported.

That did not make Darth Vader happy. "Tear this ship apart until you've found those plans," he ordered. "And bring me the passengers!"

The stormtroopers wasted no time. They had not been searching long before they spotted Princess Leia. She tried to escape, but she was not fast enough.

The troopers brought the princess to Darth Vader.

"I want to know what happened to the plans," he told her.

Princess Leia refused to speak. Darth Vader ordered his commander to take her away. He would get the truth out of her—somehow.

But the plans—and R2-D2—were about to leave the ship. They were inside an escape pod.

"You're not permitted in there," C-3PO told him. "It is restricted. You'll be deactivated for sure!"

R2-D2 just beeped at him.

"Secret mission?" C-3PO asked. "What plans? I'm not getting in there!"

Just then, another explosion
rocked the ship.

C-3PO hurried into the pod.

"I'm going to regret this," he said.

The door slammed, and the
escape pod rocketed off into space.

A short while later, the pod landed on a desert planet named Tatooine.

The plans were safe, but the droids' adventures were just beginning.

STAR WARS

THE BATTLE OF HOTH

Deep in the cold reaches of space, the ice planet Hoth orbited a pale sun. The surface of the planet was a frozen wasteland. Nobody lived there.

At least . . . nobody was *supposed* to live there. And that made Hoth the perfect place for the Rebel Alliance to hide from the evil Empire.

From the helm of his Imperial Star Destroyer, Darth Vader stared grimly out into space. He was looking everywhere for the Rebel Alliance. Vader sent hundreds of probe droids into space, seeking any sign of the rebels.

Soon the rebels noticed a droid snooping around their base on Hoth. Princess Leia hurried to the command center with Han Solo and his friend Chewbacca to discuss the droid.

"Come on, Chewie," Han told his Wookiee copilot. "Let's check it out."

The droid self-destructed before Han could capture it. But first it sent a signal back to Darth Vader. The secret rebel base wasn't a secret anymore.

"It's a good bet the Empire knows we're here," Han told Leia.

Darth Vader wasted no time. His fleet left for the Hoth system right away. They didn't want to give the rebels a chance to escape.

While Vader's Star Destroyers lay in wait in the sky above Hoth, four armored Imperial walkers began to make their way across the icy tundra toward the rebel base.

Princess Leia ordered the evacuation of the base. Most of the rebels hurried onto transport ships and left immediately. But others remained on Hoth to stand and fight. They would protect the base until everyone else had escaped. Leia stayed with them; she didn't want to leave her troops alone.

Han Solo stayed with Leia . . . he didn't want to leave *her* alone.

Meanwhile, Luke Skywalker climbed into a snowspeeder and led a squadron of fighter pilots out onto the plains of Hoth. They were going to try to fend off the monstrous Imperial walkers. Luke hoped to keep them far away from the base.

And far away from his friends Leia and Han.

Luke's squadron tried firing directly at the walkers, but it did no good. "That armor's too strong for blasters," Luke declared. So they used cables instead, tangling one of the walker's legs together.

It worked!

Luke ran underneath another walker. He fired a grappling hook into its belly and pulled himself up underneath it. Then he used his Jedi lightsaber to cut it open.

Luke threw a grenade into the walker and dropped back to the ground. *Boom!* The walker flashed with green sparks and exploded.

But even as Luke tried to keep the walkers away, the base was taking fire. The floor shook violently. Han and Leia could barely stand up! Then the alert came:

"Imperial troops have entered the base."

Han grabbed Leia's hand. "Come on," he said. "That's it." It was time to go.

Han and Leia ran to Han's ship, the *Millennium Falcon*. The golden droid C-3PO followed on their heels.

Darth Vader personally led his Imperial troops into the now-empty rebel base. As the troops searched for any signs of life, Chewie and Han tried to get the *Millennium Falcon* started. The engine revved, then choked. Steam billowed everywhere.

"Would it help if I got out and pushed?" Leia said sarcastically.

"It might!" snapped Han.

THE BATTLE OF HOTH

Han and Chewie worked furiously to get the ship running. Leia scowled. They were going to be captured by the Empire unless they could get the *Millennium Falcon*'s engine started.

Just as Han and Chewie were making their final repairs, Darth Vader
and a group of Imperial snowtroopers entered the hangar where the
Millennium Falcon was docked. They opened fire on the ship.

Han and Chewie fired back as the engine rumbled to life.

"See?" Han said.

Leia rolled her eyes.

"Someday you're going to be wrong," Leia told Han as the ship leapt into the air and rocketed out of the base. "And I just hope I'm there to see it."

Darth Vader watched angrily as the ship escaped into the sky.

Luke Skywalker watched them go, as well. He knew that the *Millennium Falcon* was the last ship to leave the base. Luke had done his job, and Han and Leia had gotten away.

The Rebel Alliance was safe once again.

RESCUE FROM JABBA'S PALACE

Han Solo was in trouble. He had been captured by Darth Vader and frozen in carbonite. The Sith Lord had then given Solo to the bounty hunter Boba Fett.

Now the frozen hero was in the one place he had desperately been trying to avoid: the palace of Jabba the Hutt.

Luke Skywalker had a plan to rescue Han. He sent R2-D2 and C-3PO to Jabba with a holographic message.

"Greetings, Exalted One," Luke said. "I seek an audience with Your Greatness to bargain for Solo's life. As a token of my goodwill, I present to you a gift: these two droids."

Jabba looked at R2-D2 and C-3PO and laughed. "There will be no bargain," he said. "I will not give up my favorite decoration."

Jabba was not about to give up the droids, either. C-3PO was assigned to work as a translator in the palace, and R2-D2 was sent to Jabba's sail barge.

Later that night, as Jabba celebrated his victory over Han, a bounty hunter interrupted the party.

C-3PO couldn't believe what he was seeing. The hunter had captured Chewbacca, the Wookiee!

Jabba was thrilled. He and the bounty hunter agreed on a price for Chewbacca, and Chewie was sent to the dungeon.

But this was no ordinary bounty hunter. It was Princess Leia in disguise!

That night, while everyone slept, she crept through Jabba's palace and freed Han from the carbonite.

"I've got to get you out of here," Leia said.

As she helped Han to his feet, an evil laugh filled the room. It was Jabba! His servants took hold of the weakened Han and threw him in the dungeon with Chewie.

Jabba kept Leia as a servant in his throne room.

The next day, a mysterious visitor arrived. It was Luke.

Using his Jedi powers, he tried to trick Jabba into freeing his friends. "You will bring Captain Solo and the Wookiee to me," Luke said. "I warn you not to underestimate my powers."

"There will be no bargain, young Jedi," Jabba replied. "I shall enjoy watching you die."

The floor opened beneath Luke, and he fell into a dark, musty pit. Luke had fallen into the lair of the vicious rancor. All around him were the bones of the monster's victims.

Suddenly, a gate opened and the rancor slithered into the pit. The beast picked Luke up in one hand and opened its giant mouth. But Luke was ready! He shoved a bone between the rancor's teeth so it couldn't bite down.

Then, rushing past the beast, he threw a boulder at the gate's controls. The gate slammed down, crushing the rancor.

Jabba was not happy. He had expected his monster to defeat the Jedi!

At Jabba's order, Luke, Han, and Chewie were brought before him.

"Jabba the Hutt has decreed that you are to be terminated . . . immediately," C-3PO translated. "You will be taken to the Dune Sea and cast into the Pit of Carkoon, the nesting place of the all-powerful Sarlacc."

As Jabba's servants seized the three prisoners, Luke looked back at Jabba over his shoulder. "You should have bargained," he said. "That's the last mistake you'll ever make."

On board Jabba's sail barge, R2-D2 slipped away from the crowd. He watched from the window as Jabba's guards prepared the prisoners. One of the guards was Lando in disguise!

Luke stepped onto the plank over the Sarlacc pit. With a nod to R2-D2, he jumped!

Suddenly, R2-D2 shot an object into the sky. Luke grabbed the plank
and sprang back onto the deck of Jabba's ship. Reaching out his hand,
he took hold of the object R2-D2 had thrown.

It was Luke's lightsaber!

Luke, Han, and Chewie wasted no time. The three jumped into battle with Jabba's men, hurling them overboard and into the mouth of the Sarlacc.

Inside Jabba's barge, Princess Leia seized her moment to escape. Wrapping her chains around the evil gangster, she defeated him once and for all.

R2-D2 zapped Leia's chains and freed her.

While Luke fought off the rest of Jabba's men, Leia aimed the barge cannon at the deck. Then, holding on to each other, Luke and Leia swung to safety.

Reunited at last, the group soared across the desert of Tatooine. Behind them, Jabba's barge exploded.

They had defeated him. But more important, they had rescued Han. They were a team again.

CHAOS AT THE CASTLE

Rey was an orphan who lived on the desert planet of Jakku. She had found the little droid BB-8 when he was separated from his master, Resistance pilot Poe Dameron. The two had become good friends. BB-8 had even shown Rey the map to Luke Skywalker that he was carrying for the Resistance. The First Order wanted the map, too, and had tried to capture BB-8. But Rey had fought off the First Order stormtroopers and promised BB-8 that she would help him get back to the Resistance. Now Rey, BB-8, and their new friends Finn, Han Solo, and Chewbacca were zooming across the galaxy in the *Millennium Falcon* to visit Han's friend Maz, who lived in a giant castle on the lush planet of Takodana. They hoped that the alien could help them get BB-8 back to the Resistance base.

Maz greeted Han and his friends with a smile and served them a big meal. When she heard they were protecting a map to Luke Skywalker, she urged them to keep fighting against the dark side. But Finn shook his head.

"There is no fight against the First Order! Not one we can win."

Finn knew the First Order was looking for them, and he wanted to run. When Maz pointed to two pirates who would take him to the Outer Rim, Finn decided to leave.

Rey jumped to her feet.

"Don't go," she begged her friend.

Finn asked her to leave with him, but Rey said no. She had promised to help BB-8 get back to the Resistance, and she wouldn't go back on her word. As Finn left Maz's castle, Rey felt something pull her toward a stone stairway.

Rey followed the stairs to a long corridor and into a dark room. She lifted the lid of a wooden box and saw a strange sight. It was a lightsaber! But when Rey touched the weapon, strange painful images suddenly filled her mind. Some were memories from her lonely past, but some were of people and places she had never seen before.

Rey dropped the lightsaber and stepped back. She was afraid.

Maz appeared and rushed to Rey's side.

"That lightsaber was Luke's," Maz said. "And his father's before him. And now it calls to you!"

Maz explained that the Force moved through and surrounded every living thing. She told Rey to take the lightsaber with her, but Rey was scared. She shook her head.

"I don't want any part of this," Rey said.

She turned and ran out of the castle and deep into the forest.

But Finn had been right. There was an enemy spy at Maz's castle. She had alerted the First Order, and the castle was under attack!

Blasts filled the sky as large black TIE fighters swarmed overhead.

Finn saw the chaos and ran back to help his friends. When he realized Rey was missing, he knew he needed to find her. Maz handed him Luke's lightsaber.

"Take it!" Maz urged. "Find your friend."

Finn nodded. He, Han, and Chewie raced from the castle to find Rey, but stormtroopers blocked their path.

Finn turned to Maz.

"I need a weapon," he pleaded.

Maz grabbed his wrist, lifting the hand that held Luke's lightsaber.

"You have one!" she cried.

Finn squared his shoulders and turned on the lightsaber. With a surge of energy, the blue blade hummed to life.

Rey skidded to a stop in the forest when a creature in a black cape and a heavy mask marched out of the trees. It was the man from one of her visions—Kylo Ren!

Kylo Ren was a dark warrior for the First Order. He'd come to Takodana to steal BB-8's map. He knew that a girl had helped the droid escape, and he wanted Rey to tell him where he could find BB-8.

Kylo's three-pronged lightsaber jolted to life. The weapon's red glow lit up Rey's face as Kylo Ren used the Force to keep her from running away.

"The droid. Where is it?" he asked.

Rey refused to give up her friend's location, but Kylo Ren sensed that she had seen the map. He carried her back to his ship so he could ask her more questions. He was determined to find Luke Skywalker.

Just then, X-wings swooped in overhead, and the stormtroopers scattered.

Another spy in Maz's castle had alerted the Resistance! Poe Dameron and the Resistance pilots had come to the rescue, and they wasted no time fighting off the First Order from the sky.

But it was too late. Kylo Ren marched up the ramp to his ship with Rey in his arms. The black shuttle lifted off and shot through the sky, carrying Kylo and Rey all the way to the First Order headquarters—Starkiller base!

As Kylo Ren's troops left Takodana, a new Resistance ship landed near the lake. General Leia Organa walked off the transport and reunited with her old friends Han and Chewbacca. But Leia's heart sank as she looked at the crumbled castle. She had spent her life fighting the dark side, and she was determined to protect her people from the First Order. She hoped using BB-8's map to find Luke Skywalker would help bring peace to the galaxy.

General Organa took Han, Chewie, Finn, and BB-8 back to her base. BB-8 and the map were safe, and the Resistance had a new mission: to save the galaxy by destroying Starkiller base. But first they had to save Rey from Kylo Ren.

Rey had been a brave friend. She had helped return BB-8 to the Resistance. Now the Resistance would help her!

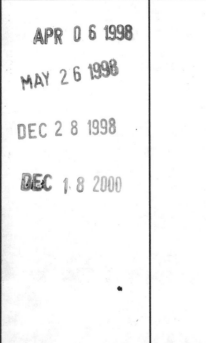

For Anne and Vincent, Isis and Mandisa—M.H.

For Kenneth, Gwen, Nanette,
and their families—C.V.W. and Y.H.

First published in the United States 1997
by Dial Books for Young Readers
A Division of Penguin Books USA Inc.
375 Hudson Street
New York, New York 10014

Published in Great Britain 1997
by Frances Lincoln Limited

Printed in Hong Kong on acid-free paper
First Edition
1 3 5 7 9 10 8 6 4 2

Library of Congress Cataloging in Publication Data
Hoffman, Mary, date.
An angel just like me/ Mary Hoffman; pictures by
Cornelius Van Wright and Ying-Hwa Hu.—1st ed.
p. cm.
Summary: An African-American child wonders why all Christmas
tree angels look alike, and sets out to find an angel
that looks just like him.
ISBN 0-8037-2265-6
[1. Afro-Americans—Fiction. 2. Christmas—Fiction.
3. Angels—Fiction.] I. Van Wright, Cornelius, ill. II Hu, Ying-Hwa, ill. III. Title.
PZ7.H67562Amf 1997
[E]—dc21 97-1428 CIP AC

The art was created with watercolor and pencil on illustration board.

★ MARY HOFFMAN ★

An Angel Just Like Me

PICTURES BY
CORNELIUS VAN WRIGHT / YING-HWA HU

Dial Books for Young Readers  New York

It was nearly Christmas, and everyone in the family was busy except for Tyler. Labelle and Marcy were putting up holly and ivy. Their mother and father were bringing in a big Christmas tree, and T.J. was sorting through the old box of decorations. Even Simone was sticking paper chains together. Tyler was the only one with nothing to do, so he teased Bagel.

"Oh no," said T.J. after a while. "Look at this angel!"

Everyone stopped what they were doing and looked at the angel. It was broken in half.

"We'll have to get a new one," sighed Mom.

Tyler picked it up. "Why do angels all look like girls?" he asked. "Can't boys be angels?"

But no one answered. "Why do they all have gold hair?" asked Tyler. "And why are they always pink? Aren't there any black angels?"

"Good question," said Dad. "There may be, but I've never seen one."

"I'm going to find one," announced Tyler. "I'm going to get a new angel for our tree. One that looks just like me."

Now that Tyler had a special job, he worked hard at it.
Every day after school he went shopping and looked at
angels. Some were big and some were small, some had
straight hair and some had curls. They all had wings.
But Tyler couldn't find one that looked like him.

And another thing—none of the angels on the Christmas cards or wrapping paper looked like him either. Some played beautiful gold harps and trumpets. Some perched on rooftops or lolled on clouds. But Tyler couldn't find a single one that looked like him.

Tyler thought maybe Santa Claus could help. At Fogelman's there was a Santa Claus with curly white hair and a beard and red cheeks that matched his clothes, but Tyler thought he couldn't be the real one. Somehow, Tyler had always imagined that Santa Claus might look a little like his own dad.

Just as Tyler was turning away, another Santa came to take over. This one wore his beard like shaving cream on his brown face. He had a huge stomach. Tyler poked him.

"Hi, Carl," he said. "Is that stomach all yours?"

"Hi, Tyler," said the Santa. "No, it's a cushion. But you're not supposed to recognize me. This is my holiday job."

Carl was an art student who was sometimes the children's sitter when Mom and Dad both had to work late. Tyler told Carl his problem.

"I see," said Carl. "I never thought about that, but you're right. You *should* be able to find angels like you."

"There's not much time left," said Tyler. "I guess if I can't find my angel, I'll just have to get a star instead. A star's the same for everyone."

On Christmas Eve Tyler's family went to church. Inside there was a Nativity scene with Jesus and His family. Animals, shepherds, and the Three Kings crowded the stable too.

"Hey," said Tyler. "That king looks a lot like you, Dad."

But the angels were just like the ones he had seen in the shops. And something else was beginning to bug Tyler.

That night, before the children went to sleep, their mother read them the story of the first Christmas again.

"So Jesus was born in Bethlehem, right?" asked Tyler.

"Right," said Mom. "Nearly two thousand years ago."

"And that's in Israel, right?" said Tyler. "And Mary and Joseph were Jewish, right?"

"Right again," said Mom. "Jesus too. They all lived in the Middle East."

"Then why doesn't the baby in the stable at church look Jewish?" asked Tyler. "He had yellow hair."

"Well, you can be Jewish and still have yellow hair," said Mom, but her head was beginning to ache.

"What about two thousand years ago?" persisted Tyler. "What did the baby Jesus really look like?"

"It's a good question," sighed Mom. "You're full of them this Christmas. But I don't know the answers. And if you don't go to sleep now, tomorrow's question is going to be, 'Where's our Christmas dinner?' Good night, Tyler."

On the other side of town Santa Claus was working late.

Christmas day was always special at Tyler's house. There were two grandmas and one grandpa, an aunt and three cousins, and even a visiting dog for Bagel to play with. It was as crowded as the stable in church. Tyler looked up at the brand-new gold star on the top of the tree and gave a little sigh.

"Stars are good," said Dad. "They are the same for everyone."

"Yes," said Tyler, "but you can see stars in the sky almost any night. They're not as special as angels."

At that moment Mom walked in with a package.

"Late delivery from Santa," she told Tyler. "This just came for you."

It was the most beautifully carved wooden angel. And—apart from the wings—it looked just like Tyler.

The next day Tyler went to see Carl and invite him back to share all the food that was left over from Christmas dinner.

"It was my best present," he told Carl. "Only now I want you to make something else."

"OK," said Carl. "What is it?"

"You see," said Tyler, "now that my friends have seen my angel, they all want . . .

. . . angels just like them!"